THE PERFECT SOLUTION

and other stories

Liz Summerson

Summerbooks

To my dear writing friend Glenis

CONTENTS

Title Page   1

Copyright   2

Dedication   3

THE PERFECT SOLUTION   7

A CHANGE OF SCENE   14

HOTPOINT JOHNNY   23

PERSONAL GROWTH   33

FRENCH FANCIES   41

SILVER LIGHTNING   49

A FINE BOUQUET   57

BEING LUCY   64

ROWS AND STITCHES   68

STIR-UP SUNDAY   74

About The Author   83

More short stories by Liz Summerson   85

THE PERFECT SOLUTION

Friends couldn't understand why, summer after summer, we kept returning to Les Amandiers.

They'd tell us about their own holidays in Tuscany and Turkey, Corfu and Cornwall, and then the inevitable remark would come. 'Don't you and Martin fancy a change? You've been going to the same corner of France for the last ten years!'

Martin and I would exchange a glance then toss out some reasons: the guaranteed sunshine of southern France, the comfortable cottage, the convenience of knowing our way around. We told them about the wonderful welcome we always received from dear Monsieur and Madame Guillemard who owned Les Amandiers. How we looked forward to seeing how the sunflowers and vines were doing and eating the luscious melons and burnished tomatoes that the Guillemards left on the doorstep. And what could beat a bottle of the Guillemards' own vintage with a simple supper of cheese, charcuterie and fruit, bought in our hesitant French from the nearby market?

Our twin daughters, Jane and Penny, chattered for weeks ahead about revisiting all the nooks and crannies of the farm, plaguing Monsieur Guillemard for tractor rides and renewing their acquaintance with the hens and ducks who gobbled up all the baguette they were offered. When the girls grew older, they, too, tried out their French – though I expect their teacher winced at the rich southern twang they took back to school.

We never exhausted the sightseeing possibilities of the area. Nearby Albi, that rose-red city on the Tarn, always enchanted us with its medieval streets, impressive historic buildings, and playful fountains where the girls loved to paddle on hot days.

Gradually we ventured further to hilltop towns with castles, glittering rivers where Martin took Jane and Penny canoeing, mysterious forests where giants seemed to have scattered boulders as casually as pebbles.

We told our friends about all these delights. But, for fear of being thought a bit crazy, we kept the strongest reason for our loyalty to Les Amandiers to ourselves.

It centred on the Visitors' Book. In this large, blue volume, each set of guests described their week or fortnight's stay, telling the next residents where they'd been, what they'd eaten (and drunk) and generally what an amazing time they'd had.

Most people wrote really helpful stuff, like which was the best market for olives and the opening times of various attractions. Some showed off, the Mum or Dad desperately creating pen-pictures of the perfect family: everyone always in a good mood, revelling in cultural outings and with the sharpest possible noses for the True French experience, whether in the local Leclerc supermarket or at the many vineyards offering wine tastings. It was fun when the children sneaked a last sentence in, contradicting what their parents had written.

On our first visit to Les Amandiers I spent much of the first evening poring over the entries, chuckling at the self-satisfied tone of some and the human honesty of others. The final piece in the book had been added that very morning by the Saunders – Henry and Jill from Windsor. This couple had, they said, been coming to the cottage for six years. I'd noticed Henry's previous accounts, distinctive by being in real ink. From his style, I guessed he was a recently-retired professional: a teacher or lawyer, maybe. But the Saunders were as anonymous as all the other writers until I read their latest entry.

'Jill is still packing.' Henry had written. 'Why does it take her such an age? Why must she bring so much? Surely one skirt, two tops and a supply of paper pants would do! And so many books!'

I chuckled at his grumpy-old-man ranting but smiled in a different way at his next sentence. 'We shall be so glad to return next year as, quite simply, we LOVE this place.' Then, to my surprise, I found he was addressing us directly. 'Madame Guillemard tells me there's a family with children coming here today. So here's a little puzzle for you people. Where does the fish jump over the bell? Clue: it's not more than 2 km away. Have a lovely holiday.' A different hand – evidently Jill's – had added, 'I hope you will love Les Amandiers as much as Henry and I do, and that you will long to come back next summer.'

In those few words, Henry and Jill stopped being anonymous. Only that morning, I realised, they'd breakfasted on the terrace where I was now sitting. They'd cooked all fortnight on the fierce-looking Calor gas stove, showered in the blue-tiled bathroom, and slept comfortably – so they mentioned – in the old oak bed which Martin and I were about to share. And, thoughtfully, they'd left us a message and a puzzle.

That year, the twins were eight years old: just the age to enjoy Henry's challenge. On and off throughout the week we returned to it.

'A fish jumping over a bell?' said Jane. 'Let's find a river.'

But the map showed no river within two kilometres.

'What about the pond by the barn?' Penny suggested. They rushed off to the pool that Monsieur Guillemard used for irrigation but trudged back reporting no luck.

'Perhaps it's a feature on a building,' said Martin, getting as intrigued as the girls. 'Something to do with a doorbell, maybe.'

We walked down to the village and peered carefully at every building. Though we didn't find a fish jumping over a bell, we saw all sorts of things we might otherwise have missed. Quaint dovecotes barely visible from the road, door-knockers that British antique dealers would kill for, gargoyles and corbels that you'd swear had been modelled from the faces of the villagers sitting in the square. At last, one afternoon when we'd all piled in the car to go to the supermarket, Penny spotted it. Shading her eyes, she pointed across the fields. 'That church has got a bell,' she said, 'and I can see something shining above it.'

'Where?' squealed Jane.

Penny bounced up and down, tapping the window. 'There! Go there, Daddy.'

Excitement rose as Martin headed the car down the nearest lane. Drawing close, I sighed along with the girls as we all looked up to see, perched above the bell that hung in its framework of stone, a golden weathervane in the form of a leaping fish.

'Let's set Henry a challenge in return,' said Penny, as we celebrated with raspberry icecreams and Orangina.

'That'll be hard,' I warned. 'He knows this place inside out.'

'We'll think of something,' said Martin.

Which we did, writing it in the Visitors' Book on the last morning of our holiday.

'Now we'll have to come back next year to see if he solves it,' said Jane.

This thought diverted us from the sadness of saying au revoir to the ducks and chickens and to Monsieur and Madame Guillemard, who saw us off with a round of cheek-kissing and a bulging bag of fruit.

But it really was only au revoir: we had already made our booking for the following year.

Henry didn't disappoint us. We returned to find he had solved our challenge – 'but only with much difficulty and pleasure', he wrote – and he'd set us a new one. 'A bit harder, now that Penny and Jane are nine.'

And so it went on, Henry and Jill becoming penfriends with whom we corresponded – only once a year – through the Visitors' Book at Les Amandiers. Each time, Henry wrote: 'We'll be back next year, if we're spared.' And his next entry always began,' Well, we were spared – it's wonderful to be here again.'

The challenges continued, becoming increasingly sophisticated until they read like cryptic crossword clues. Through the puzzles, Henry opened our eyes to that wonderful area. The girls still took an interest, to humour us, but it became a quirky Mum-and-Dad holiday thing, rather than theirs. Finally, when they were 18 and just finishing their A levels, they made a not-unexpected request. 'We're too old for family holidays. Can we go to Ibiza with the gang?'

So that year we set off alone, rattling about in the car which was no longer packed to the roof with all the girls' caboodle. It was a parched summer. There were warnings of water shortages and an odd sense of doom seemed to haunt the air. Construction work for a new road near Limoges even caused us to lose our way.

'Everything's changing,' I murmured to Martin. 'I'm not sure we should keep coming back now.'

'Wait and see. You can bet Les Amandiers won't have changed. And,' he smiled and stroked my thigh, 'there are some advantages to not having the girls with us, however much you're worrying that they're OK.'

I nodded. He was right. And I didn't have to struggle too hard to resist the temptation of phoning the girls, because they soon texted to say they were having a great time.

Martin was right, too, that Les Amandiers hadn't changed. The Guillemards looked a little older but were as welcoming as ever, full of questions about the girls which I more or less understood and did my best to reply to.

'But poor Monsieur et Madame Saunders ...' Madame Guillemard's face clouded. 'It is very sad...'

I felt my heart thump. 'Henry and Jill? What's happened? Not ill, or...'

'Non, non .... you will see in the book. Now, I leave you to unpack. A bientôt.'

I dropped my suitcase where I stood, snatching the Vistors' Book from its familiar place on the sideboard. I could hardly bring my-self to open it, but I needed to discover what Madame Guillemard meant.

'Dear Sue and Martin, Jane and Penny ...' Henry had used his usual fountain pen. 'Thank you so much for the last challenge. It took two trips to the Toulouse-Lautrec museum, but we finally cracked it, and I wouldn't have missed a last look at Lautrec's paintings for anything.' I frowned. 'Unfortunately,' he continued, 'this must be our last trip to Les Amandiers. We have become too doddery to manage the drive again. We are both over 80, you know.'

We hadn't known. I'd imagined them as lively 60-somethings. Tears prickled as I read on to the last sentence: 'So it's farewell – no longer au revoir – to this dear place that we have loved to visit for fifteen years. When you come again, as we're sure you will, please say hello to everything here for Henry and Jill Saunders of Windsor.'

Henry had set us no challenge that year. Without it, and without our lovely daughters, Martin and I felt at a loose end. Though the cottage was small, it felt empty without the girls. I glanced into the bedroom they'd always used. Fresh white bedspreads were spread tightly over the twin beds and no clutter of makeup and hairbrushes untidied the dressing table. Mealtimes were for-lorn without their chatter and without one of Henry's challenges to solve. We couldn't consume half the produce that the Guille-mards left us, though it was no more than usual.

'Maybe this should be our last time, Sue. Time to move on?' Martin said tentatively.

I'd been halfway to broaching it myself. The Guillemards, too, had hovered round us on tenterhooks all week, unvoiced questions on their faces.

My lip trembled. 'We've loved it here so much.'

'I know.' Martin stroked my hair. 'But without the girls, without Henry and Jill...'

'It's so ridiculous,' I mumbled. 'The girls have to grow up, and we've never even met ...'

I hesitated as a thought sprang into my head, then looked up to find Martin's gaze meet mine.

'Sue?'

'I think,' I said slowly, 'that Henry's subconsciously set us a last challenge after all,'

And that is how I came to be ringing a Windsor number that Madame Guillemard rooted out of an envelope stuffed with bits of yellowing paper.

'Mr Saunders?' I said into my mobile. 'Henry? This is Sue. I'm calling from France to ask how would you and Jill feel about a trip to Les Amandiers next year.'

After all, with a half-empty car and an empty twin bedroom, wasn't it the perfect solution?

A CHANGE OF SCENE

The battlefields of northern France are a funny place to try to mend a marriage. But when Paul suggests a long weekend, I can't think of a good reason not to go.

'We can take the car through the Tunnel,' he says. 'This weather's going to hold and it will do us goo to get away, Annie.

I shrug. ' As long as we agree to be nice to one another.'

'Sure.'

Paul teaches history. Visiting the battlefields is something he's wanted to do for ages. As for me, anything's better than another silent weekend in the London heat.

I pretend to sleep for most of the journey. But once we reach Arras, Paul is keen to get going. Map in hand, he leads the way to the huge town square that has been so perfectly reconstructed, you can't tell the tall Flemish houses were once shelled to bits. We go beneath the houses into strange underground caverns and passages. A guide tells us how the people of Arras once stored their wine and cheese here and even held subterranean parties. But in the war, they used it as a hospital. There are plenty of photographs to prove it. Nurses who could have been me, soldiers who could have been Paul.

'How about a walk in the park?' suggests Paul when we emerge. 'You've probably had enough about the war for now.'

He's right. But, with an undeclared war of our own still simmering, we're both on edge as soon as there is nothing specific to do. We watch each other like cats. Although it's not been said, we both know that pretty soon the crunch is going to come.

Although it's not been said ... That, of course, is where the trouble lies. We haven't been communicating properly for months. We're no longer on the same wavelength.

Our first night in Arras doesn't go well. Oh, nothing wrong with the hotel. It's a former monastery, cleverly converted. But over dinner, we rack our brains for things to say, then leave our meal half-eaten. We go to bed early, then spend the night each clutching an unfriendly edge of the double mattress where once we'd have cuddled in the middle like spoons.

Today, given half a chance, I'd have headed for home. Not that home seems much of a description now for the house we did up so lovingly only three years ago. But Paul's determinedly ploughing on with his itinerary.

'Shall we go to Amiens this morning, Annie?' he says at breakfast. 'Or Lille? The shopping's better, I expect.'

I'm shrugging again – it seems to have become a habit – when the waiter interrupts.

'Excusez-moi, Madame, Monsieur, but you have no choice. You must go to Amiens.' He smiled. 'It is my birth-town. You must visit the Cathédrale and the hortillonages. They are marvels.'

Despite myself, I return his smile. 'I've heard the Cathedral's special, but what are the hortillonages?'

'I will not spoil your surprise, Madame,' he said. 'You will discover it yourself. And today is perfect.' He gestures at the bright sunshine pouring through the dining room windows.

I see Paul is nodding as though he knows what the waiter is talking about.

'Paul...?' I begin.

'Let me show you, Annie. You won't regret it.'

An hour or so later, we are gazing at the interior of the magnificent Cathedral. The brochure claims it's the best in France and it could even be true. The medieval woodcarvings that cover the choir stalls are so old, the wood is almost black. The craftsmen's skill demands reverence, but the ancient faces are full of personality and humour.

I point to a miserable-looking individual, the spitting image of our postman at home.

'And that one's just like old Mac from the newsagent's,' Paul says, almost laughing. I realise it's been a long time since I heard him laugh properly.

When we come out of the cathedral, the sky has unexpectedly clouded over. It might even rain. Nevertheless, we follow the signs to the hortillonages along a footpath that leads us past attractive riverside buildings.

Then, suddenly, we are in a breathtaking world where a network of artificial islands spreads before us. We start to explore the footbridges between the islands. There are little pavilions and lush gardens. Dense weeping willows hide strange boats that are curved like miniature gondolas. Everything is so green, a thousand shades of green. We walk slowly. It's like treading through a dream as, all around, the water makes a gentle murmur. I feel calmer than I've felt for a long, long while.

'How did you know about this place?' I ask Paul. 'Have you been here before?'

'Never,' he says. 'But it's in that book by Sebastian Faulks. Birdsong. Some people picnic here.'

'Well, it's amazing,' I reply. 'I love the peacefulness. And what's the river?'

'The Somme.'

As soon as he says those two little syllables, it's all spoiled. Everyone's heard of the Somme. Such an innocent-sounding name, but such a horrible symbol of death and destruction. I shiver, almost expecting the water to contain traces of blood.

Paul seems oblivious to my reaction.

'Talking of the Somme,' he says, 'I'd really like to see some of the First World War sites. Do you mind, Annie? I'll go on my own if you want to go shopping.'

I suppose he's trying. Perhaps that's why I agree to go. Battlefields have never been my idea of a day out. But now my sense of peace has been shattered, I'm almost feeling masochistic. I start to walk fast back towards the entrance to this place.

'Hey, no need to try to break the world record,' Paul calls after me. 'We've got all day.'

L ater, after miles of open countryside, Paul stops the car. We follow a track that climbs high above the roadside. Though the sky is oddly misty, it's hot and I am glad to flop down on the grass. We eat the picnic stuff we bought in Amiens – baguettes, Brie and pâté. Or at least Paul tucks in. Apart from his munching, we are surrounded by silence.

Paul's been buried in his guidebook for ages. Every now and then, he brushes the crumbs off, looks up to peer intently at the landscape, then goes back to the book again.

'What are you looking at?' His preoccupation irritates me where once I would have smiled fondly at it. I can see nothing special in the scenery. It's just miles of crops and grass, khaki and ochre in this hazy light.

He lowers the book and looks at me. 'This place is like us, you know.' He gestures at the fields.

I raise my eyebrows and sigh. There he goes again. Trying to be intellectual about our problems.

'You and me,' he continues, ignoring my rebuff, 'we're like the poor blinking armies of the First World War. Sniping at each other week after week, year after year, even though they'd practically forgotten what started the war. If they ever really knew. They'd advance a few hundred yards, fight like crazy, pick up their dead, then get forced all the way back. Over and over again. One side got the upper hand, then the other, then back to square one. They destroyed everything in sight in the process.'

I take in what he says, then reply carefully. 'I thought the World War One slaughter was all the generals' fault. Their bad decisions sacrificed so many lives. Well, there are no generals controlling us.'

He frowns. 'Sometimes it feels like there are. Our jobs pull us in different directions. No time to be together. We're always running round in circles, trying to cram everything into too few hours. It's caused all the bickering...'

'We let it happen. We didn't set our own priorities. Perhaps we didn't even...' I decide against continuing. 'Oh, look, the sun's coming out.'

Instantly, everything is bathed in gold. I feel the warmth on my arms. If only our relationship could be warmed as simply, as quickly.

I notice that Paul is staring towards the fields beyond the road. Surely he hasn't disappeared into his own little world again. But then he exclaims.

'There! I see it. Zigzagging, look.'

'What are you on about now, Paul?' I snap, but nevertheless my eyes follow his pointing finger to a line of almost-flat grassy curves in the middle distance. They weren't visible before but, in the sudden sunlight, their contours are illuminated bright-green. They interlock like sections of a plaited loaf.

'It's an untouched trench,' he says. 'One that was never filled in. It's described in the book but I couldn't see it until the sun came out. The land's recovered all by itself over ninety years. Now there's barely a scar. Isn't that fantastic?'

Despite myself, I'm moved. My mind replays that sepia newsreel they show on TV now and then. Silhouetted figures, helmeted, carrying rifles, climbing over the trench tops to their certain death. Soldiers' bodies have nourished this soil. No wonder the grass is so lush. But it's taken ninety years to turn all that mud and blood back to green velvet.

I don't even know if any of my own ancestors fought in the Great War. But, confronted by the thought that trench warfare took place right here, my eyes fill. I almost grab Paul's hand.

'How could something so awful have happened here? Where it's so calm?'

He shakes his head. 'I know. Unimaginable, isn't it? There was a substantial wood over there, the book says, where they fought for five days until not a stick remained.'

'The wood never recovered, then.'

'Not everything can.'

I stare at the picnic remains then start to tidy up.

W e drive on to the next village where, in the scatter of houses, I glimpse a hand-painted sign. 'Look, Paul!'

He pulls in. 'What is it?'

'Back there. It said Musée de Guerre. War museum.'

'It'll be a rip off. Some old codger with a few bits and pieces trying to cash in on battlefields tourism.'

'I'd like to look, all the same.'

He looks surprised. 'OK.'

We get out of the car and walk back. The museum is just a corrugated lean-to, tacked on to a cottage wall. Inside the doorway, an elderly man sits on a kitchen chair, watching the world go by. He raises his hand to us.

'Bonjour, Monsieur,' I say. 'The musée - it's yours?'

'Oui.' His weather-beaten face cracks into a gap-toothed smile. 'Vous êtes Anglais.' He's not asking but announcing. 'Come inside. I find all these remains from the Guerre in the fields nearby. Souvenirs. You can buy them.'

'Told you so,' whispers Paul.

The shed is lined with crude shelves spread with dingy pieces of twisted metal, green with verdigris, rusted with age. Some are distorted beyond recognition. Others, I can see, are bits of helmets, guns, grenades, shells. There are more personal objects, too: a mess-tin, a pocket knife, buttons, a bent pair of spectacles with its lenses intact. Further along lie a few bleached bones, a fragment of a jaw.

The man indicates a small rectangular tin. 'This came up in this year's ploughing. There is always something, every spring, every autumn.' Though well-rusted, the lid carries the ghost of a picture.

'Ah,' says Paul, with interest. 'I know what that is. Queen Mary's Christmas gift for the troops. She sent chocolate to every soldier.'

The Frenchman's eyes gleam. 'You are right. But it does not contain chocolat now.' He turns the tin on its edge and I see marks where he must have forced it open. 'Inside,' he says,' was this papier.'

It's a folded yellow fragment, almost falling apart at the creases. Most of the looped writing has faded. It's too dark in the shed to make it out. I take it carefully to the doorway, then read aloud:

"... socks next parcel ... pray you come home safe, my darling Edward. Milly sends kisses ... your mother says ..."

'That's all. My lip quivers. 'But he wouldn't have got home safe, would he?'

Paul shrugs. 'Impossible to say. He might have just dropped his tin. But, no, he probably didn't make it back. One of the thousands and thousands who died here.'

To my surprise, he clinks the coins in his pocket.

'How much?' he asks the old man.

They agree a price and, taking the handful of euros, the old man hands over the tin.

'Merci. Bonne journée,' he says. 'Ave a good day.'

Outside, I take the tin from Paul. The metal is warm from his hand. Once it was warmed by Edward's.

'Poor Edward,' I murmur.

'Poor girl who loved him,' says Paul. 'Poor everyone. So many pointless battles ... such a waste of life and love.'

He frowns, looks searchingly at me, reaches to wipe a tear from my cheek.

'Are you OK, Annie? Are we OK?'

I hold his gaze. 'Let's make it OK, Paul. I really want to, if you do. We have something worth hanging on to. This little tin, this whole place... they've given me a sense of perspective. We don't have to fight.'

And when he puts his arm around me, it feels so good as we walk away together in the sunshine.

HOTPOINT JOHNNY

'I must be the last woman in town still washing by hand.'

Mum's arms were full of wet laundry. There were damp patches all over her pink bri-nylon overall and her flushed face almost matched it for colour.

Dad looked up from his paper. 'You've got a good mangle...'

Mum threw a dripping sock at him. 'I'll mangle you! You've no idea how hard it is turning that handle. And that's after I've scrubbed my hands raw. Not to mention rinsing and bluebagging. It's even worse now than with the old copper and I'm not doing it any more. I want a twintub.'

We'd moved into town a few months previously, just before my tenth birthday. We were forced to quit our tied cottage when Dad's boss sold the farm. Dad had found work in town and, thanks to some money Gran left us, we'd just been able to afford our terraced house and a bit of modernising.

'You don't know the meaning of mod cons,' Mum muttered.

She was right. Twelve years older than Mum, he didn't.

'You think I should be satisfied with an inside lav and one power-point in each room.' She was getting into her stride.

He put his paper down on the kitchen table. 'There's the electric cooker. And the telly,' he said, defensively. 'You like that new pro-gramme. You know, Coronation Street.'

'Yes, I do. But perhaps you've noticed even Elsie flippin' Tanner has a twintub,' said Mum. 'I'll get a job myself and buy one on easy payments.'

'I won't have you working,' retorted Dad, 'or our Susan being a latch-key kid. And we'll get nothing on the never-never. I only buy what I can afford outright. What do they cost, anyway?'

Mum grabbed the now-damp paper and pointed to a large advertisement.

'That lovely Hotpoint,' she said. 'It's not that much. I've already saved fifteen pounds from the housekeeping.'

'So that's why I haven't seen a decent chop in weeks,' Dad snorted. But it was his final grumble. 'I'll see if I can get some overtime,' he mumbled, escaping into the garden.

Mum pulled a face at his back before turning to me.

'He's so old-fashioned,' she said. 'Take my advice, Susan. Don't marry an older man.'

I t was the school summer holidays when the twintub arrived. Once I'd helped Mum remove its cardboard packing, the machine filled the kitchen with a smell of newness. Together we admired the gleaming white metal and the blue-grey worktop that lifted off to reveal the two tubs that gave it its name.

'One for washing, one for drying,' Mum said, knowledgeably.

'What do all these letters around the knobs mean?' I asked.

'I don't know,' said Mum. 'The shop's sending the demonstrator this afternoon. She'll show us everything when she comes.'

I was thrilled I was going to be there.

However, the demonstrator turned out to be a man, and quite a young man at that.

'The name's Johnny.' He grinned, showing perfect teeth.

I knew what Mum was thinking. So, it was plain, did he.

He stroked his chin. 'You might be wondering what a man knows about washing. But I'm an engineer. Believe me, I know all there is to know about washing machines, Mrs Jenkins.'

'It's Brenda,' Mum simpered, fluffing up her hair with one hand. I could see she wished she'd used the Rose Geranium lipstick that she kept in the sink-unit drawer.

Johnny slipped rubber hoses over our taps and whooshed water into the machine's shiny innards. Then he produced a tiny packet of Daz and asked for some laundry to use in the demonstration.

Mum nudged me. 'Get those towels from upstairs, Susan. The ones on the bathroom chest.'

'But...'

'No buts, young lady,' said Mum firmly, though I'd only been going to say that those were already clean and there'd be more point doing Dad's overalls.

I clattered upstairs, grabbed the neat pile, and thundered down again, only to bump into Mum at the bottom.

'Help me crumple them,' she hissed, 'so they look used.'

I followed Mum back to the kitchen, where Johnny, checked shirtsleeves now rolled up over hairy forearms, stood over the steaming tub.

'Just pop it all in, Brenda, as the actress said to the bishop.'

Mum giggled. I was surprised. Mum wasn't given to giggling and I didn't think he'd said anything very funny.

'Now I start the agitator,' he continued, rotating his hips and pulling a face, 'and while the washing cycle's on, we can have a brew. If you don't mind making one.'

Mum got out the best china, and she and Johnny laughed and

joked as we watched the Hotpoint slurping the washing around. Eventually the agitator stopped and he lifted out our towels with wooden tongs.

'See how much cleaner they are!' he said, transferring them into the spin-dryer.

I knew why Mum bit her lip. However much she hated hand-washing, her results were always immaculate.

'And ...' he wagged his forefinger, 'when you fill the dryer, remember this rubber mat must go on top of the load, with your smalls right at the bottom where they belong. Because if they're very small' – he winked – 'they'll go over the edge and clog up the works.'

The dryer roared into action and the whole machine lurched as a torrent of grey water poured from the tube hanging over the sink.

'I bet you're thinking you should've had a twintub years ago,' Johnny said. 'I hope your husband doesn't take you for granted.'

Mum blushed. 'Not at all. We've only just moved from the country. We didn't have electricity there.'

'Oh,' he smirked. 'A country girl? That explains the lovely complexion.' The last drops of water went down the plughole. "Over to you now,' he said. 'Pegging it out is definitely women's work.'

Mum was beaming.

'Sure you'll manage on your own next time?' asked Johnny.

Mum nodded. 'Quite sure, thanks.'

'If anything goes wrong, anything at all,' he said, patting Mum's shoulder, 'ring the office and I'll be round.'

Then he ruffled my hair and was gone.

hen Dad came home that evening, Mum was still busy washing everything she could find. There wasn't a spare inch on the clothesline, but her eyes were shining.

'Pleased then, old girl?' said Dad. 'Easy to use, is it?'

'Simple as ABC,' Mum replied. 'The engineer came. He showed us everything.'

'A feller? Sounds like a nancy boy.'

'What's a nancy boy?' I asked.

'Never you mind,' said Dad.

All went well for a week or two. Dad wore a clean shirt daily, instead of making one last two or three times, and we all benefited from that. It no longer mattered if I got mucky playing, because everything went straight in the twintub. Mum looked much perkier and her hands became soft and pink.

Then came the day when Mum went shopping and I was at a loose end. I knew it was wasteful filling the twintub just for my teenage-doll Mandy's clothes, but I could do some washing for Mum as well: I'd look in her Ali-baba basket.

I tipped in the last of the tiny packets of Daz that Johnny had left and put everything in the washtub. While the machine performed, so did I, mincing about the kitchen in Mum's shoes. I pinched some Rose Geranium lipstick from the sink-unit drawer, working my lips together like Mum did. I backcombed my hair and made myself a cup of tea.

At last, it was time for the spin. Into the dryer everything went: I switched on and the motor whirred. But though I realised both my mistakes almost immediately, it was already too late. First, water flooded from the hose which I'd forgotten to hook over the sink. Then everything juddered to a standstill. My heart sank. I hadn't put the rubber mat in the dryer. I'd tried to spin items which were far too small, and now I'd broken the machine.

Scared, I wiped off the lipstick and mopped up the flood: a minor one, as at least the tiny garments hadn't held much water. But I'd broken Mum's precious twintub. The sky was about to fall in.

When Mum returned, her first reaction was to shriek. But when she'd cooled down, she said, 'Johnny did say he'd fix any problem. Though if the guarantee won't cover it, heaven help you.'

She dragged me to the phone-box. I stood outside while she made the call.

'He's coming tomorrow afternoon,' she said, when she emerged. 'Dad's working late, so we should get away with it.'

I lay low next morning, dressing and re-dressing Mandy in her freshly-laundered things. They'd come up really nicely, but I mourned the ones lost in the spindryer - a chiffon ballgown, a pink tank-top I'd knitted. Would I get them back?

At dinner-time, I noticed Mum was wearing a new skirt, make-up and high-heels. She must be going shopping later: perhaps I'd go with her. We'd just washed up when the door-knocker went.

'That'll be Johnny,' said Mum, reaching for the sink-unit drawer. 'You let him in.'

I walked slowly to open the front door.

There stood Johnny in another checked shirt, holding his tool-box.

'Hello, princess. Spot of bother?' He winked.

'Come through,' Mum called.

I let him pass and crept out into the garden, lingering on the back doorstep long enough to hear Mum say, 'I'm so sorry, Johnny – it was Susan, washing her doll's clothes. The spinner's jammed.'

'Don't worry.' To my relief, he sounded cheery. 'Good excuse to visit, eh? Now, let the dog see the rabbit.'

From the kitchen, occasional laughter reached my ears. At least no-one was cross, then. After a while, wondering how Johnny was getting on. I peeped through the kitchen window. Mum had her back to me, leaning against the cooker. Johnny was bent over the machine and, as I watched, he extracted from the dryer first my doll's ballgown and then Mum's bra.

Horrified, I burst in, trying to snatch the items, but he held them teasingly above my head. Mum blushed, though all she said was, 'Oh, Susan!'

'It's mine!' I shouted. 'Give it to me.'

Johnny laughed. 'You're a nice girl to try to spare your Mum's blushes,' he said, 'But this'd be a bit big for you.'

He stretched out Mum's bra, making the lacy cups dance and bulge between his hairy-backed hands. Then, tossing it to Mum, who coughed delicately, he reached into the spindryer to retrieve a tiny, misshapen piece of pink knitting.

'I wonder what this is meant to keep warm?' he said, in a silly voice.

'It's my doll's jumper,' I shouted, grabbing both it and the ball-gown and rushing outside.

'Johnny!' I heard Mum remonstrate. Then there was silence. Then, a giggle. It seemed a long while before the front door banged and the van drove away.

Mum called from the backdoor. 'Susan!'

I didn't answer.

'Susan! We're going to the shops. Now.'

Reluctantly I went indoors. The kitchen looked as it always did, the twintub tucked away in the corner, its formica worktop back in place. Mum combed her hair, reapplied her lipstick and powdered her flushed cheeks.

'Sorry, Mum,' I mumbled.

'So you should be. You didn't mention my undies were in with your dolls' clothes. I've never been so embarrassed.' But she didn't look very embarrassed.

'Thank goodness it wasn't my winter drawers.' She reached for the wicker shopping basket. 'Well, everything's fixed now, and without your Dad knowing, thank goodness. Come on!'

We walked down the street to the local shops.

'We'll get something nice for Dad's tea,' said Mum. 'Keep him sweet. A tin of red salmon, I think.'

Ahead of us, chatting outside the grocer's, I could see two women I recognised. I didn't know their names, but I knew they lived at the top of the street. As we approached, one of them looked at us and nudged the other.

Mum smiled. 'Nice day, ladies,' she said, brightly.

'Very nice,' replied the younger of the two. 'I noticed the Hotpoint van outside your house earlier. Trouble with your washer? Needed seeing to?'

The older woman tittered.

'Yes,' Mum frowned. 'Madam here forgot to use the mat when she spun her dolls' clothes in my new twintub.'

The first woman smirked. 'Hotpoint Johnny fixed it, did he?'

'Yes. Most efficiently.'

'Johnny's certainly very efficient.' She looked at her friend. 'We've all got Hotpoints round here.

'We all rely on Johnny,' said the other, putting her hand on the handle of the grocer's door to push it open.

There was a pause before Mum spoke.

'Indeed,' she said at last, her voice suddenly cold. 'Come along, Susan.'

She pulled me away from the shop, head high, her face as red as her lipstick. We marched into the butcher's.

'A piece of rump steak, please,' she said. 'The best you've got.'

'Treat for your hubby, eh?'

Mum smiled tightly.

'He deserves it,' I said. 'He's the best dad in the world.'

The butcher beamed. 'He's a lucky man to have such a lovely family.'

He packed the meat into a brown-paper parcel which Mum thrust into her basket. As soon as she'd paid, she grasped my arm and rushed me all the way back up the street.

'Slow down, Mum!' I protested. 'I've got a stitch in my side and your fingers are digging in.'

But she didn't stop until we were home, the door clacking sharply behind us. Then she leaned against the passage wall, panting. I tried to pass her, but she caught my shoulders.

I yelped. 'Mum ... what's the matter? It's fixed. Johnny fixed it.'

'Shut up!' she rasped. Her chest heaved and spittle bubbled at the corner of her lipsticked mouth. 'It's all your fault this has happened, Susan. Don't you ever go near that twintub again. Do you hear? Never!'

She released my shoulders, stooped and slapped the backs of my legs three times, very hard. My calves stung, but my heart stung even more: she had never before smacked me. She had never before been unfair.

'Now,' she said, 'get upstairs. And don't you dare tell your Dad that anything happened this afternoon.'

'Nothing did happen,' I sobbed, running to my bedroom.

From the window, I saw the two women walking slowly by below. They looked at our house and sniggered.

'Nothing happened,' I whispered.

I hated Mum at that moment. Even more than I hated Hotpoint Johnny. But it was Mandy I took it out on, snatching her from the bed and scribbling with a biro all over her simpering face and naked conical breasts. Later – days later – Mum scrubbed her with meths and Vim. But I could always see blue scars where the pen point had dug in.

And that's what I learned from that day.

There are some things you simply can't mend.

PERSONAL GROWTH

G ood jobbing gardeners are hard to come by. Once found, however, they become part of the garden furniture. They arrive, they get on with their work, they pack up at the end of the day. Generally, they don't merit a second glance.

Which is how Kate got away with it.

She dressed suitably for the role - baggy T-shirt, jeans, sunhat and wellies – yet, if you'd asked her employers, could they have described her?

'Oh, she's quiet and sensible,' they'd have started, confidently. 'Mousy hair. Long or short? I'm not too sure. But definitely no make-up. And medium height, I'd say.'

It was the gardens of four adjoining houses in Cranbrook Close that Kate tended, but none of the owners realised their gardener was also working for the other three. Their high hedges encouraged standoffishness. Most residents could recognise the others in the street but either because they'd never having been formally introduced, or because they weren't really interested, they passed without speaking.

When Mrs Ada Williams from Number 2 collided with Miss Millicent Bradshaw of Number 8 in the library, each merely muttered, 'So sorry' and carried on her way (though each also glanced nosily at the other's books and Millicent, juggling her walking frame and her large-print romances, tutted at Ada's thrillers). And when Arthur Tennison (Number 4) spotted young David Fox (the newcomer at Number 6) in the bank, he studiously ignored him. As for David, he was too preoccupied to be interested in his neighbours.

Strangers rarely visited the Cranbrook Close houses and nor did friends or relations, for that matter. But Kate had simply marched up each long path to offer her gardening services. To her gratification, all four householders had sound reasons for saying 'yes'.

Ada had devotedly tended her dear Ernest's garden ever since his death, but now it was too much work. Retired bachelor Arthur preferred penning detective stories to pruning and weeding and busy David Fox had neither time nor enthusiasm for gardening.

Millicent, frail and arthritic and genteelly poor, was delighted at Kate's modest charges. 'I've been so worried about neglecting the old place,' she said.

So Kate began putting the four gardens in order, allocating each a specific day from Monday to Thursday. The residents readily agreed to giving Kate cash payment (they could leave an envelope in a flowerpot, if they wished) and carte blanche with designing and planting.

Her Fridays, Kate devoted to her other job.

Around the corner in Linden Grove stood the doctors' surgery where everyone in Cranbrook Close was registered. It was a go-ahead practice, offering chiropody and physiotherapy on the spot. The partners had even taken on a part-time counsellor recently. Very much part-time: in fact, Fridays only.

Yes, you're right. The counsellor was Kate, quite literally in another disguise. On Fridays, she turned into the well-spoken Ms Katherine Wingate, wearing neat suits, medium-high heels, spectacles, subtle but full make-up, and her brown hair twisted into a smart chignon. Quite unrecognisable as the jobbing gardener.

In contrast to her gardening gear, the counselling outfit made Katherine look her thirty years. This was deliberate: the role demanded gravitas and Kate's first-class degree in psychology qualified her to judge what her clientèle would expect.

She had taken a postgraduate diploma in counselling largely to please her parents, who pooh-poohed her passion for gardening and the effort she'd put into gaining horticultural qualifications part-time.

'Hardly a profession, dear,' they said.

Luckily, the counselling course proved unexpectedly enjoyable and it was always useful to be dually-qualified.

'Personal growth and plant growth are not unrelated,' she told herself.

It was not long before, one by one, our Cranbrook Close residents made their way to Kate's counselling clinic.

First, Ada referred herself. Since Ernest's early death, she had been deeply lonely. But she told Kate how she felt guilt-ridden at hoping to find another companion for her remaining years.

'I shouldn't contemplate replacing Ernest as though he were a pet poodle, should I, Ms Wingate?'

'Do call me Katherine, please.' said Kate. 'Now, Ada, think what missing Ernest so much says about your relationship with him.'

'I suppose it shows how important he was to me, which is why my life is empty without him,' said Ada.

'That's an enormous compliment to him,' Kate said gently. 'Hardly disrespectful, is it?'

Ada nodded thoughtfully.

'Perhaps you should broaden your social relationships,' suggested Kate. 'There's a new afternoon club at the Linden Grove Social Centre with bridge, tea-dances, sing-songs and such. You could make some friends. It's worth a try, don't you think? Let's talk more next Friday.'

'Thank you, dear,' murmured Ada. 'You're very wise.'

Next came Arthur. In a low sad voice, he explained how life was passing him by. Since retiring from the town hall, he'd grown tired of writing his whodunits (all, he admitted, unpublished). He sounded just like Ada when he said how lonely he felt.

And, just as she'd said to Ada, Kate suggested the Social Centre might be a tonic.

'What about your neighbours?' she asked. 'Do you get on with them?'

He shook his head. 'We keep ourselves to ourselves in the Crescent.'

'But perhaps,' offered Kate, 'you all lack friendship, tucked away behind your front doors. Think about it.'

'I will, my dear,' said Arthur, half-saluting her as he rose.

David, consulting his GP about insomnia, was referred for counselling with underlying stress queried. It didn't take him long to admit to Kate he'd been recently jilted.

'I haven't been able to talk to anyone about it before,' he said. 'You're very easy to open up to.'

'Talking's generally better than tablets. But is your work overstressful, too?'

David sighed. 'Yes, but it's my own fault. I've become a workaholic. It seemed a salvation.'

'You must cut down,' said Kate, more firmly than counsellors usually do. 'Why don't you spend time just relaxing in the garden?'

David brightened. 'I might just do that,' he said. 'Since I've had a gardener, I've noticed it's actually worth sitting in.'

'There you are, then. Good luck!' Kate showed him out.

When Millicent was referred by a community nurse, Kate diagnosed social isolation compounded by immobility.

'Even going to the library is getting beyond me,' Millicent confessed.

'You need 'books on wheels',' said Kate, 'and perhaps a few mobility aids. Incidentally, there's a new social club along the road. I could arrange a lift so that you could try it.'

'Oh, I don't mix much. I can't...'

'No such word as 'can't'. You could you mix more,' asserted Kate in a voice that brooked no argument.

'Very well, I'll try.' The smile was brave. 'You know, you do remind me of someone, Ms Wingate.'

'Oh?' Kate flushed. Had she been discovered?

'It's my old nanny,' said Millicent. 'She always said there's no such word as 'can't.'

M eanwhile, throughout that long spring, Kate worked hard on the Cranbook Close gardens. She had a plan for each plot and, with the free hand accorded by the householders, she was unstoppable.

At Ada's, she tidied the rockery, re-edged and trimmed the lawn, then dug a long narrow bed in the middle. This, she filled with lobelia. Arthur's shrubs next door needed only a light pruning. She replanted his borders, then, in his lawn, she cut a ring-shaped bed.

'I'll plant it with begonias,' she remarked, collecting her day's pay.

'What about a hydrangea in the middle?' Arthur ventured.

'No. Definitely no.'

'Oh well - you're the gardener,' he chuckled.

'Good to hear you laugh,' she said. 'Life looking up?'

'Indeed,' said Arthur. 'That social club has given me a new lease of life. D'you know, I met my charming next-door neighbour there. Ada Williams. She's ... delightful.'

David's garden was more challenging, especially since he some-times turned up in the afternoons, wanting to chat. Kate always wore sunglasses although, since he'd only been twice for counsel-ling, she felt fairly safe. She opted for pinks and mauves for his gar-den - rather feminine, perhaps, but he wouldn't be alone for ever. With her penchant for central flower beds, she made his chevron-shaped, planting it with dianthus to flower all summer.

For Millicent, she chose old-fashioned scented roses and, in the lawn, a curving flowerbed which she filled with pansies.

'That's an unusual shape,' said Millicent, as she waved goodbye to her books-on-wheels volunteer.

'It's a little joke,' said Kate, gruffly. 'Gardens should be light-hearted.'

'I'll give it a closer look when get my mobility scooter next week,' Millicent confided.

'Terrific,' said Kate, keeping her head down.

'No stopping me then!' Millicent laughed, shutting the door.

When all the gardens were flourishing to Kate's satisfaction, she went – in her counsellor guise – to the Linden Grove Social Club. There, she found Ada and Arthur sharing a settee and having tea with Millicent.

'Why, it's Katherine from the surgery,' cried Ada. It was some while since Kate had seen any of them for counselling, but they greeted her like an old friend.

'Since we've got to know one another, we've discovered what a help you've been to us all, dear,' beamed Ada.

Kate feigned surprise.

Millicent joined in. 'So silly, letting ourselves become prisoners in our own homes. Life has picked up no end since we've broken out.'

'Coincidentally,' added Arthur, 'we realised we also all employ the same gardener. Girl called Kate. D'you know her?'

'Possibly,' said Kate vaguely. 'But listen: I want to invite you all to a hot-air balloon trip over the neighbourhood.'

Millicent clapped with glee. 'How marvellous!' Then she bit her lip. 'Will it be expensive? Since I splashed out on my scooter ...'

'It's my treat,' Kate smiled. 'Do say yes.'

So, one glorious Sunday in July, the five of them - Kate invited David separately - clambered into the balloon's basket. The canopy swelled and the pilot announced lift-off. Soon, they floated high, eagerly seeking landmarks beneath them.

'There's St Mark's ... and the fire station,' said Arthur.

'And this is Cranbrook Close,' cried Ada. 'But ... what's that in the gardens? Surely it's a word?'

'It's 'love'! Millicent exclaimed. 'Look what our little gardener's done! She's spelled out the word 'love' in our flowerbeds. One letter in each garden. We couldn't see it at ground level.'

Across the balloon basket, David gazed at Kate. She found his blue eyes magnetic. Suddenly, she realised that, with him, her game was up. But as he started to speak, she put a finger to her lips. The others noticed nothing: they were still marvelling at their gardener's ruse.

'What an odd thing for her to do,' said Arthur, 'and yet how apt. This summer has brought love and friendship into our lives.'

'Yes.' David said, still looking meaningfully at Kate. 'All our lives.'

'Oh,' cooed Millicent. 'I detect romance in the air! Mr Fox and our dear Ms Wingate!' She beamed at David and Kate, as Kate blushed and they both smiled helplessly.

And that was really the end of that - or, rather, just the start. Two weddings took place that autumn. David's and Katherine's whirlwind courtship thrilled the older residents, who welcomed her amongst them. Arthur, having moved postnuptially into Ada's home, let Number 4 to students, who enlivened the Close considerably. Millicent in no way envied all this pairing off, preferring her romances on paper, and her gentlemen at arms' length, as at the social club's bridge sessions, where she'd made such delightful new friends.

The only person they missed was Kate, who unaccountably disappeared around the time of the balloon flight.

'Nice lass,' said Arthur, when they were all having coffee with the Foxes one morning. 'Good gardener, too. What made her go off, I wonder?'

'She was always rather mysterious,' ruminated Ada. 'We didn't even know her surname. She could be anywhere by now. What do you think, Katherine?'

'Who knows?' said Katherine, shaking her head and holding David's hand very tightly indeed. 'With my counsellor's hat on, I'd say she had probably been seeking some personal growth. But who knows?'

FRENCH FANCIES

The Eurostar burst through the Tunnel into northern France.

'We'll be in Paris in an hour!' Fifteen-year-old Lilly sighed in anticipation.

'But remember I did say you won't see much of Paris,' her mother Sally reminded her.

'Why not?'

'As I told you, Vaumont-les-Ormes is virtually a suburb, though they don't like the term.'

'But we are going to Paris first, aren't we?' Frowning, Lilly re-arranged her various layers of black clothing.

Her father Roger spoke with his eyes closed. 'We'll see as much of Paris as we saw of London. In other words, the inside of the Gare du Nord, which will be just like Saint Pancras International.'

A pity he wasn't sitting with some of the other rare men in the party. They could have formed a splinter group. It was mainly the wives who were the Francophiles. Especially Sally who, as chair of the Westmarsh Twinning Association, had insisted on a family turn-out for what she threatened would be 'a weeRogerd to remember.'

Getting the twinning underway had taken Sally immense time and effort. Now her hard work was about to reach fruition, with the actual charter ceremony taking place later that very day. Coming late to the game, it hadn't been easy finding a sibling for Westmarsh. All the picturesque towns in Normandy and Brittany had been snapped up by early birds, and when the international twinning bureau had tentatively, and desperately, proposed Vaumont-les-Ormes, Westmarsh had not felt immediate enthusiasm.

'It's hardly an identical twin!' the secretary of the Westmarsh committee had protested, looking at Vaumont-les-Ormes's town brochure. 'What does our little town have in common with all these five-storey apartment blocks?'

'I know,' Sally had replied. 'But we've been searching for two years now. Let's at least give Vaumont-les-Ormes a try. Maybe opposites will attract.'

Grudgingly, the committee had conceded. Next, there were speculative visits during which, as parties in any arranged marriage, they'd eyed each other first covertly, then more boldly. Eventually, it looked as though things could gel, but Sally admitted that even now, at the eleventh hour, her one remaining worry concerned someone she had not yet met: the mayor of Vaumont-les-Ormes, Henri Beaupoireau.

The French side had dropped hints. 'Not an easy man' was the consensus. Noted for his pride, rather than his bonhomie, Beaupoireau's lantern-jawed portrait adorned every item produced by the town hall's publicity department. Mayor for many years, he seemed to see his job as repelling boarders - which perhaps explained why there'd been no town twinning to date.

'It ees true that Monsieur Beaupoireau is wary.' Pierre Marchand, the charming twinning chairman on the French side, had shrugged his shoulders and pursed his lips. 'But ee will be zair on ze day.'

Sally had shrugged and pursed back: it was catching, this Gallic response. Then, finalising arrangements through a hectic couple of months of cross-channel emailing, she'd put the problem of Beaupoireau to the back of her mind.

'Ee will be zair,' Pierre had repeated only the previous evening, skyping to given the programme a final check.

Roger was enjoying being swept along at 186 mph. He reflected that it might, after all, be fun to get to know some foreigners and it was good to see Sally so happy. He opened an eye now to give her a fond look. But why on earth was she rummaging at his feet?

'Don't say I've forgotten the spoons!'

'Spoons?'

'Yes - there are three dozen silver-plated ones with the Westmarsh crest. Mementoes to give out to worthy citizens of Vaumont-les-Ormes.' She delved further into her bag until something clanked gently. 'Thank goodness, here they are.'

'How will you decide who deserves one?' Roger was genuinely puzzled. 'Have you agreed a code of winks amongst the committee members?

'Don't be so silly, Roger.' Sally used the same tone to put down the ten-year-olds she taught as her day job. 'We shall just ... know.'

'Where's the big present, Mum?' Lilly asked. 'That picture of the Town Hall?'

'The Mayor's got that. Mr Porter, the butcher. He's travelling first class to be more dignified. The framers wrapped the picture beautifully - I didn't want it looking like a parcel of meat. But I do hope the French don't notice the bus stop.'

'What bus stop?' Roger and Lilly spoke together.

'Didn't I say? The picture's a nineteenth century scene, but history wasn't the artist's strong point - h's painted in that the bus stop that's in front of the Town Hall. And the litter bin.'

'Oh, Mum!' Lilly used the superior tone in which fifteen-year-olds specialise, and shook her head. 'That's so naff. Wake me up when we're in Paris.'

Naff or not, everything else was working like clockwork. The train arrived punctually and Sally rounded up her flock, while Roger rushed down the platform to help their puffing mayor with his luggage.

If Beaupoireau was a man of Gallic reserve, Westmarsh's Billy Porter was a very different kettle of fish. He took his one-year office of mayor very seriously even if he had neither much intelligence or confidence to bolster him in the role. Still, Sally reflected, despite his red face, today he looked quite ... dignified: indeed, he'd worn his chain of office around his broad, butcher's shoulders all the way from Westmarsh, so as not to be mistaken for just anybody.

The French welcoming committee standing in the archway didn't look like just anybody, either. All six of them sported blue baseball caps with bold union jack and tricolor motifs. Doffing his, Pierre Marchand advanced towards Sally. She never knew whether he'd stop at three kisses or go on for four but, having somehow avoided bumping noses, she was at last able to introduce the bashful Billy Porter, who was all geared up to say the Bongjoor that he'd been practising for months.

'So where's their mayor?' he asked.

Sally looked around.

'Monsieur Beaupoireau n'est pas ici?' Sally enquired of Pierre.

'Mais non. But ee will be zair,' he replied firmly, as he started to launch a noisy round of handshakes, 'bonjours' and 'enchantés'. It was only when the gift of a baseball cap had been pressed - literally - on to each English visitor, that the group began to move out of the station towards the awaiting coach.

'Well,' Sally said brightly, 'At least the hats will ensure we don't lose anyone.'

Lilly winced, powerless to escape a middle-aged Frenchman determined to position her hat at just the right chic angle.

'Magnifique, Mademoiselle!' He surveyed his artistry. 'Ze perrrfect Engleesh rose! Eef only I 'ad ze camera.'

'Thank God you haven't,' Lilly muttered darkly.

'Well! He deserves his spoon!' Roger felt genuine admiration for the man's outmanoeuvring of his daughter, who now flounced to the back of the coach.

It was a good half-hour's jouney to Vaumont-les-Ormes. Heads rotated, as features of the passing scenery were pointed out. Sally attempted a translation of Pierre's rapid-fire French, but several old ladies protested that neither their ears nor arthritic necks could cope. Roger sympathised but, stoically, he nodded and smiled, giving a convincing impression of being engrossed in every detail.

Eventually, Pierre announced, 'Zees ees where Paris ends and Vaumont-les-Ormes starts. Voilà'.

No-one could tell the difference, but it seemed polite to cheer.

The coach drew up at the flag-bedecked Mairie and, as the English party descended, a bridal group came out.

'Fancy! Just like an English wedding,' one lady remarked, eyeing the confetti, the over-tight and over-embellished outfits of the women, and the men's discomfiture at the clicking cameras.

Her friend sniffed. She'd read up about Vaumont-les-Ormes.

'Fifteenth century, this town hall,' she confided. 'Used to be where some king's mistress lived.'

'And now they use it for marriages? I'm not sure that's very nice.'

Pierre, hovering nearby, caught the word 'marriages'. 'Les mariages, ladies, like our twinning - a marriage between our towns, yes? And it ees to the marriage room where we go now.'

Everyone smiled and nodded. The wedding group moved away, stamping the butts of their Gitanes underfoot. Pierre ushered his guests indoors and up a sweeping staircase to the magnificent marriage room, where apéritifs, canapés and various VIPs from Vaumont-les-Ormes awaited them.

As the Westmarsh party headed for the refreshments, Sally scanned the assembly. Some, she recognised from her previous visit; others, she was less sure about. She smiled ambivalently at everyone, then touched Pierre's arm.

'Monsieur Beaupoireau?' she murmured.

Pierre shook his head. ' Be patient. Ee rests after ze wedding ceremony.'

At one end of the huge room, small gold chairs stood in rows facing a large table flanked by French and British flags. Above it, the President's photograph. Sally hoped fervently that everything was in place for the signing. At least their gift - the picture - was propped ready against the wall, as splendid in its red, white and blue wrapping as any French paquet-cadeau, yet somehow nonchalantly British in its pose.

As the clock moved towards five, everyone sat. Ninety minutes of sipping apéritifs had done wonders for the entente cordiale, though not for aching ankles. However, even Lilly, monopolised by a dashing young Frenchman, now looked remarkably cheerful.

Then - nothing happened. People shuffled and whispered. It seemed ages since Billy Porter, visibly nervous, had been pushed through a door by Pierre. Sally, passing the time spotting potential spoon-receivers, looked again at the clock: twenty past. Was Beaupoireau in there? Was someone ill? What was going on?

'Bride's prerogative,' whispered Roger.

Sally was not in the mood for jokes. Surely a just impediment wouldn't emerge? In her head, she heard Pierre's insistent 'Ee will be zair.'

Suddenly, the Marseillaise struck up. Everyone stood as Beaupoireau materialised majestically before them, gesturing towards Billy Porter to join him from the wings. God Save the Queen played tinnily, then Pierre motioned the audience and Billy Porter to sit.

Beaupoireau remained standing and, fixing his audience with an imperious stare, began to speak. He was resonant, he was impressive. Even those who understood no French applauded enthusiastically: clearly, the banal English translation that followed, read out by Pierre, did no justice to the original. Then it was over to Billy Porter. He waited for Beaupoireau's nod before, red-faced and anxious, he said 'his little word'. A teacher from the Westmarsh comprehensive, trying not to sound like De Gaulle, translated it into French and led the polite clapping.

The charter was signed with fountain pens and flourishes. The anthems were played again. Then Pierre announced:

'An' now, ladies and chentlemen, ze geefts.'

Beaupoireau and Porter swapped rectangular packages. Simultaneously they removed ribbon and layers of paper. Sally watched as Porter won the unwrapping race, halting Beaupoireau temporarily in his tracks as he held up a kind of neo-cubist-impressionist interpretation of Vaumont-les-Ormes's town hall.

Lilly gulped beside Sally, as Porter spluttered in English.

'Well, Monsieur Beaupoireau, that will look champion in our civic foyer. Thank you most kindly on behalf of the citizens of Westmarsh.'

The clapping had barely died when Beaupoireau resumed his task. Grim-faced and with precision, he cast aside the last sheet of tissue paper, then took such a sharp intake of breath that everyone in the room heard it, even the deaf ones.

Oh no! Roger squeezed Sally's hand tightly as she flushed to the roots of her hair. He'd seen the bus stop!

Gazing fixedly at her feet, she missed the first view of Beaupoireau smiling like no-one had seen him smile before. A stiff crinkle spread across his face and remained, even when he tried to cough it away.

Slowly he turned the picture to the audience.

At the gasp that went round the room, and the nudge in the ribs from Lilly, Sally could not help but look up.

And saw not Westmarsh town hall . Not the anachronistic bus stop and litter bin. But a nude. A roly-poly, luscious, ripe and rosy, female nude. With cherries, though not in all the strategic places. And, in her hand, a very large leek. Whatever had the framers done? Oh, mistake of all mistakes!

Beaupoireau was speaking again. In English. More English than anyone knew he knew.

'Zees leek ...' he paused dramatically, 'Zees leek honours my name. In Eengleesh, 'beau poireau' means 'andsome leek. And zees lady oo 'olds ze 'andsome leek, she ees magnificent. I sank you all. I was ... wary. But I like your Eengleesh sense of 'umour. I seenk zees twinning will be more fun zan I 'ad ever sawt. And not just for ze young people but for everyone.'

And amidst the cheering that erupted, no-one heard Sally say faintly, as Pierre urged her forward to shake Beaupoireau's hand:

'I think he's going to be worth a spoon after all.'

SILVER LIGHTNING

A s I let myself into Nan's flat on Friday, I hear her television booming as usual. She's deafer than she admits so I call loudly.

'Hi, Nan!'

'That you, Ellie?

'Who else would call you Nan except your only grandchild?'

'Steven calls me Nan.'

Steven's my ex-boyfriend. We drifted apart six months ago but he still visits Nan, which only encourages her belief that he's the ideal husband for me.

I give her a kiss and change the subject. 'So how are you today?'

'Pretty good, love. But what about you? I hope you're not working too hard.'

She worries about the fact I've gone back to college at twenty-seven. Says too much studying could cause brain tumults. True, my life is pretty tumultuous, juggling part-time jobs and my degree course. But I'm trying to make something of my life.

'I know you'd rather I found a man for a meal ticket,' I tease, 'but I'm fine, Nan. And you of all people should back me.'

'Of course I do.' Her chin juts stubbornly. She knows I'm well aware that she raised my mum alone rather than marry someone she didn't love. And that was back when unmarried mothers were social outcasts. 'But all this female emaciation's going too far,' she protests.

'Emancipation, Nan.'

'That's what I said. It's the men that need liberalising now you women are foraging ahead on every front. Take Steven ...'

'I don't want to take Steven.' I keep my tone light. 'I'm very happy with Gregory, thanks.'

And I am. He is sophisticated and gorgeous, my new bloke.

Nan sniffs. 'I don't trust him. A wolf in cheap clothing, that one.'

Nan's only met him once and she behaved appallingly. She told him he needed a haircut, managed to splash his silk tie with tea, and kept singing Steven's praises. Fortunately, Gregory merely thought she was batty. Which she certainly is not, but I shan't rush him into a repeat performance. And that's sad because, now that my parents live in Spain, Nan's my only family here.

'Anyway,' I say, 'Steven's surely got another girlfriend.'

Nan neither confirms nor denies this. 'He fetched my prediction from the chemist,' she says. 'In his lunch break. Nice boy. Always asks about you.'

'Nice boy' accurately sums Steven up. He works in a DIY shop, hoping he'll become manager one day. His idea of splashing out is a take-away and a rented DVD. Gregory, on the other hand, works in advertising and his smooth car, platinum credit card and Italian suits have already accompanied me to a couple of very romantic restaurants.

I try to divert Nan. 'Are you still on the same tablets?'

She chants the litany: 'Blue ones for blood pressure, yellow for colostrum and the white diabetics for my water. Trouble is, I forgot to ask Steven to buy corn-pads and I'd like to go to the Club tomorrow night.'

Clubbing for Nan means a rave-up of bingo and waltzes at the Over-Seventies. But her troublesome corns are legendary.

'I'll bring some on my way to meet Gregory tomorrow,' I offer.

'Oh, would you, love?' She brightens. 'Now switch that nonsense off,' she nods at the television, 'and I'll make tea. Let's have muffins. Don't know about you, but I'm ravishing.'

Ravishing is exactly how I plan to look tomorrow night. Gregory's taking me to the opening of the latest Cochon Bleu restaurant. He's masterminded their advertising campaign.

'Wear something stunning,' he's instructed. 'It's an extremely important evening.'

I desperately hope he'll like the strappy black dress that I couldn't really afford. Against my better judgement, I've brought it to show Nan.

'What d'you think?' Taking the garment from its carrier bag, I hold it against me. 'Imagine sheer black tights, kitten heels ...'

Nan nearly chokes. 'That's never a dress! It's a petticoat. It's almost a bloomin' vest.'

'Don't you like it?' I say. 'I think Gregory will.'

'I don't doubt,' Nan hmmphs. 'You'll be flouting all you've got.'

'Flaunting, Nan,' I say automatically as I refold the dress. I might have known she'd disapprove, but I'm still disappointed.

On Saturdays I work at a call centre.

'Polyflex Incorporated. How may I help you?'

I parrot this so often, my brain numbs. I try to focus on the escape-route from this robotic existence that my degree will provide. But my mind keeps wandering to the evening ahead with Gregory.

On the way home, popping into the chemist's for Nan's corn-pads, I'm tempted by the tiniest bottle of my favourite perfume. No change from £20, but what the heck?

I'm to make my own way to the Cochon Bleu as Gregory has to be early to sweet-talk the foodie journalists. I shower, do my make-up and spray myself lavishly with the perfume before slipping into the black dress. Before buttoning my coat over my exposed flesh, I gaze at my reflection. If this doesn't wow Gregory, nothing will.

It's only when I get to Nan's with the corn-pads that I realise I haven't transferred her key to my evening bag. Bother. I like to spare her the trouble of letting me in, but there's no alternative. I press the bell and hammer on the door.

'Nan!' I yell. 'I haven't got my key!'

But she can't seem to hear over the TV. Thank goodness my mobile's in the evening bag. I dial her number – but there is no answer.

Perhaps she's in the loo. Or getting dolled up for her club. How can I make her hear?

I push the flap of the letterbox inwards and the TV blares out even louder. I call through the open slot, then take a look. With no light in the hall, it's hard to make anything out. Then my heart thumps. I can see something small and pale in the doorway that leads to Nan's bedroom.

I think it's Nan's pink slipper.

TV cop shows make it look easy to shoulder a front door open. I brace myself and try a couple of times, wincing as I bounce off ineffectually. No good knocking up Nan's neighbours – she doesn't leave spare keys with anyone. 'I'm not having open sesame for every Tom, Dick and Harry,' she says. Never mind that Nellie and Lil next door are little old ladies like herself.

I see no alternative to dialling 999.

'Police,' I say, praying an ambulance won't be necessary.

Waiting for help to arrive, I keep trying Nan's phone and calling through the letterbox. The slipper doesn't move.

An interminable half-hour passes before the police car arrives. Then in microseconds the broad-shouldered officer assesses the situation and bursts Nan's door wide open.

'Stay there,' he orders me, running towards Nan's bedroom.

Next thing – to my huge relief – I hear Nan shriek.

'Who the devil are you? One of those strippergraphs? Ellie's idea of a joke?'

'Nan!' I almost trip over the slipper in her bedroom doorway. 'Thank goodness you're OK.'

Nan is lying on her bed, dressed in her best Lurex cardigan and pleated skirt. Still muzzy from sleep, she's furious to be caught without what she calls her 'indentures'.

The policeman's talking really nicely to her, but she won't have it.

'Ellie!' she hisses. 'Tell him to clear off.'

I sit on the bed beside her. 'I couldn't make you hear, Nan. I didn't have my key.'

'I was having a nap,' says Nan, crossly. She's put her teeth in now. 'I wanted to feel fresh for this evening. Next thing I know, I'm waking up with the SOS all over me.'

'Shall I make some tea?' the officer suggests, tactfully ignoring Nan's ungraciousness. 'You've both had a shock. And shall I turn that TV off?'

The tea calms Nan down but, when she realises her door's been forced, she's very huffy. She gives the policeman such a dirty look that, showing him out, I apologise profusely.

He smiles. 'She's bound to feel upset. I'm only glad it's a false alarm.' He fingers the broken doorjamb. 'If you've any trouble finding someone to fix this, or you or your Nan would like advice on security, let me know.' He takes a card from his pocket. Handing it to me, he notices my get-up. 'You look as if you should've been somewhere nice tonight. What a shame your evening's spoilt.'

I thank him and shut the door as best I can. Looking at my watch, my heart sinks. It's far too late for the Cochon Bleu do. Anyway, I couldn't leave Nan's door like this.

'That copper gone?' Nan comes to view the damage.

'Don't worry. I'll get it sorted. But first I must ring Gregory. He'll be really worried.'

My mobile shows a dozen missed calls and text messages from him. With the ringtone always switched off, because of work and college, I haven't even noticed.

Guiltily, I call him. 'Gregory, I'm so sorry, but don't worry, it's OK...'

'OK? I don't think so! Why the hell aren't you here?'

The harshness of his voice stuns me. 'But ...'

'But nothing. I'm standing here on my own like a right prat.'

'It was Nan. An emergency ...'

'You knew this was my big night, Ellie. How could you do this to me? Why didn't you answer your phone?'

'Gregory, listen...'

'Forget it.'

He cuts me off. I stare at my mobile. How can he not even want to know if Nan's OK? Turning, I find her standing behind me.

'Ellie, your big date,' she says. 'I'm sorry, love.'

Her hearing's worked this time, then. Almost as well as her instincts about Gregory.

I swallow hard. 'It's OK, Nan. Just don't say I told you so.'

I start deleting all the messages Gregory's blasted at me. After the display he's just put on, I've no intention of reading them. And certainly not of seeing him again. One further zap will delete his number for good.

I riffle through my stored numbers. That's when I flick past another familiar one. But of course...

'Nan? Steven will mend the door for you, won't he?'

'He doesn't work in DIY for nothing and I guarantee he'll be here like a shot.. But it's you he'll do it for. He's never stopped holding a cauldron for you.'

'Candle, Nan.'

'Why d'you want a candle? The electric's working.'

I hug her. She is priceless.

'Look,' I say, 'I'll ring Steven and see if he's free. But you can put your corn-pads on and go gallivanting at the Club as planned. I'll stay in for Steven.'

Nan claps her hands with glee. 'Of course, love. I'll not play goose-berry. And take your coat off. Steven could do with a shock to his statistics.' Evidently, she hasn't forgotten the strappy dress. 'I know he's not very ... ' she purses her lips. 'But you'll perk him up with that outfit.'

'Nan! You're incorrigible.'

In a moment, I'll ring Steven's number. After Gregory's nastiness, it will be brilliant to hear his voice. But, if he is free to come round, my coat is definitely staying on. Despite Nan's hopes, Steven and I aren't right for each other. He deserves someone who'll really appreciate him.

Anyway, to my own surprise, there's already a glimmer of light on the horizon. And all thanks to Nan – though, naturally, she hasn't a clue.

Am I awful? Apart from his name (which his card says is PC Rob Miller) all I know is that he's kind with a decidedly sexy smile. Of course, I may have got it wrong, but I'm pretty sure he's hoping I'll contact him. And not just for advice.

Meanwhile Nan issues a parting shot as she goes off to don the corn-pads.

'Silver lightning,' she says.. 'It lurks behind dark clouds, Ellie, ready to brighten your life.'

'Surely you mean..?' I start to say, but she's out of earshot.

Which doesn't matter because, muddled or not, Nan's words suddenly sound good to me.

I cross my fingers and murmur them like a charm.

Silver lightning. I hope it's about to strike.

A FINE BOUQUET

The paper cone of flowers lay bang in the middle of the aisle leading to the exit of the multi-storey. Karen stopped her Ford Ka abruptly and jumped out to look. She could have crushed them to bits and what a shame that would have been! But where had they come from? Who would just abandon a bunch of flowers?

Finders, keepers. She scooped them up and tossed them on to the passenger seat as she scrambled back in. Then hearing a couple of impatient beeps behind her, she slammed her door shut and moved off. A glance as she refastened her seat belt confirmed carnation buds. Definitely not her favourites. She'd had too many guilt-ridden garage bunches from Pete, her ex-husband.

But Gran always said, "You can't beat carnations for lasting," And, since Gran was her next port of call, what luck! She wouldn't arrive empty-handed after all.

Carnations certainly had a better survival record than Pete's promises: to give her enough housekeeping, to keep out of the pub, to be faithful ... but she didn't want to think of Pete. It was too nice a day as she drove out of Bath towards Eastview Heights Retirement Home. Blue sky, golden sunshine. It felt fantastic to be her own woman on a day like today.

The only good thing to come out of her marriage was Laura. And if, for the last eighteen months as a single mum, Karen had been pretty hard up, that wasn't much different from when she was married.

She parked the car outside Eastview Heights and went to find Gran, who beamed predictably as Karen kissed her and presented the bouquet.

"Carnations! Thank you, Karen, love! They'll be gorgeous when they come out and they'll last so well. But you really shouldn't have."

"My pleasure, Gran," Karen replied. "I'll get a vase"

She didn't like deceiving Gran, but she couldn't admit she hadn't bought the flowers.That she couldn't have afforded them. She didn't want Gran to know how broke she was. The £200 she'd just forked out to get her old Ford Ka through the MOT - and then she'd had to find a ridiculous £6 for the car park that morning.

Not that she'd ever have gone to the multi-storey if there hadn't been a last-minute hunt for school trip money. ("Yes, Mum, it's got to be in today. Miss said!"). Then - oh joy - roadworks had sprung up overnight all along the A4 into Bath. Karen had watched the clock on the dashboard glide relentlessly onwards, leaving her no choice but to swap her usual cheap Park'n'Ride for the multi-storey. Otherwise she'd have been impossibly late for work. Wait-ressing wasn't much of a job, but at least it fitted around Laura's school hours and more or less paid the bills. She just had to hope she'd find something better one day.

As she arranged the carnations in Gran's vase, Karen didn't worry where they'd come from. They might well be guilt flowers, dropped by someone who probably deserved to lose them, but to Gran they were gorgeous flowers. That was all that mattered.

"Now, Gran, wait till you hear what Laura did yesterday.'

'Road hog! What a stupid way to drive in a multi-storey!'

Melanie had to slam on the brakes of her pink Mini Cooper as a blue 4x4 shot out right ahead of her, going the wrong way down the aisle. Her handbag, phone and paper-back romance plunged to the floor while the offending vehicle hurtled towards the exit like a getaway car.

Suddenly Melanie remembered the notices all around the carpark warning about car theft. Apparently it happened all the time these days. What if someone just pinched that vehicle? Should she ring the police?

But there would be little point: she hadn't seen any of the jeep thing's registration plate through its insolent cloud of exhaust fumes. Upset, she began to move off.

But after only a couple of yards another holdup was staring her in the face. A battered old Ford Ka had stopped dead ahead of her, blocking the way to the exit barrier. Tutting, she watched the driver get out and bend to pick something up from the roadway. Then, as the woman straightened, Melanie had her explanation.

Flowers! People might call Melanie too fanciful, but she could certainly put two and two together and knew a rejected love offering when she saw one. That jeep driver must have hurled the bouquet through window, so upset or angry that they wouldn't have cared which way the arrows were pointing.

Melanie's imagination had sprung fully into action. She thrived on relationship crises - well, other people's - and if only she could have been the one to retrieve those flowers, she knew they would have told her more. Now it was too late. The driver of the old Ford Ka had got back into her car with the bouquet. How infuri-ating was that, when Melanie desperately wanted to confirm that the flowers were the dozen red roses she pictured. There might be a card with them, which would explain more of the story. Now she'd never know.

As she gripped the steering wheel in frustration, she inadvert-ently leaned on the horn. Another driver added a beep of his own and the Ford Ka quickly moved off. Melanie sighed. But, emerging from the concrete underworld into the bright Bath sunshine, she recognised that the incident had brightened her afternoon even if she had been left with a story half-told.

As she eased into the town centre traffic, her spine tingled with pleasure at the prospect of curling up in the garden hammock with a bar of dark chocolate and a long cool drink to read 'Tender is the Day',. She couldn't wait to find out how Cassandra would get herself out of that situation on the Eurostar with Lawrence Treherne.

It beat housework any day.

D an swerved the borrowed blue Subaru jeep into a space near the gates of Victoria Park and checked his watch yet again. Of course, after rushing so frantically, he was now early. But he had been desperate not to keep Vanessa waiting on their first proper date.

He'd hated the drive through Bath, what with roadworks, the new one-way system and the grumpy-old-man irritation he felt for city traffic now he lived out in the Somerset sticks. What made it worse was that, because his Rover had engine trouble, he'd had to borrow the jeep-thing from the local garage. A real bucking bronco, and he'd met some in his army days. Still, it had got him here in one piece, so he should be grateful.

As long as Vanessa showed. She wouldn't stand him up, would she? No, of course not. When he'd phoned her – very hesitantly – she'd said yes, she'd love to do the matinée at the Theatre Royal.

"But why don't we meet earlier?" she'd suggested. "How about the Botanical Gardens? They're lovely at this time of year."

He pictured her warm smile and blue eyes, toffee-blonde hair that fell in a shiny curve. He made a face as he caught sight of himself in the mirror. Vanessa must be at least ten years younger than his

49 years, and he looked every day of his age. Nothing he could do about that though, he told himself philosophically as he got out of the vehicle.

Oh – mustn't forget the flowers. It hadn't occurred to him to buy any until he'd spotted that display as he was nearing the city centre. Suddenly, it seemed an omen that there was a perfectly-placed multi-storey so that he could stop and get some. Vanessa might expect flowers. Would be sure to like them, anyway, as she'd suggested the Botanical Gardens.

Dan had thought the paper cone of carnations would do nicely. He'd dismissed the hand-tied lily-things as too flashy and the red roses as presumptuously romantic. Not that he was well up in the etiquette of dating. His experience was limited. And would have remained so if it hadn't been for that dinner-party where he'd met Vanessa.

He opened the rear door of the jeep to get the bouquet. But where was it? Frowning, he lifted the linen jacket that he'd tossed on to the seat. He hadn't crushed them, had he? No? Fallen on the floor, then?

His heart sank as he pictured himself standing by the Subaru, annoyed as he realised he'd have to go back and put the parking token through the paying machine at the other end of the building. He replayed the scene further. He must have put the flowers on the roof of the jeep while he rummaged through his pockets for coins. Then, worried about running late, he'd accelerated away, the unfamiliar gears jerking.

Now he'd not only no flowers to give her, he'd nothing to occupy his arms that could only swing soldier-fashion when empty-handed. Worse, there was no distraction from the butterflies fluttering in his stomach.

The Park was beginning to bustle with children and parents coming from school. As Dan strode along, following the signs to the botanical garden, his path was crossed by a father laden with discarded school tops and bags whilst his boys chased across the grass after the squirrels. Lucky bloke! Dan might have enjoyed having kids himself, but fate dealt him a different hand the day Sally jilted him nearly twenty years ago. Still, he'd been a devoted godfather to the sons of several friends.

As for marriage, he'd been too hurt by Sally to risk heartbreak again. Of course, he'd had girlfriends now and then. But he'd made sure he never got too involved. The army had been his family. The army didn't let you down. And, seeing the marriages of too many of his fellow officers and men crumble under the strain of military life, he felt he'd been wise to stay single.

It was only since retiring that he'd felt rather lonely. Tucked away in the Mendips running his internet military history bookshop, he'd become a bit reclusive apart from trips to the post office. That must be what his neighbours had noticed, inviting him to that dinner-party. The one to which they'd also invited Vanessa.

He hadn't liked the idea of being set up and doubted she did either. But he had to admit he found Vanessa enormously attractive. They really had seemed to click immediately. At the same time, the idea of – how could he put it? – 'getting serious' made him feel incredibly nervous.

He was still thinking how ridiculous that was for a man who had faced battles and bullets in various locations around the globe, when a familiar voice startled him from behind.

"Dan! Slow down. It's far too warm to walk so fast!"

Turning, he saw Vanessa.

"I've been trying to catch you up all through the Park!" she said. "Ever since you locked up that wonderful vehicle you were driving. But you've been stomping along as though you were on a route march."

"I'm so sorry ... I've never learned to stroll." He raised his arms in an apologetic gesture that reminded him of what he had intended to be carrying. "I meant to bring you flowers," he blurted out, suddenly imagining the paper and petals and stems now squashed by car wheels to unrecognisable mush. "I even..."

But she interrupted him, reaching to kiss his cheek then gesturing at the colourful flowerbeds glowing in the sunshine.

"Flowers? Aren't there enough here?" she said.

In the warmth of her smile and the scent of her light perfume, Dan experienced a sudden flutter that felt really good. He'd such a lot to learn, a lifetime to catch up on, and now was the time to start.

Flowers would have only got in the way.

BEING LUCY

I f you'd asked her colleagues at the estate agency, they'd have said Lucy was sweet and helpful. But no-one would ever cite courage as one of her strong points. Faced with conflict, Lucy always backed down first.

At home, she'd make do with the trickling shower (which she hated) rather than oust the tiniest spider from the bath. At work, she inevitably got lumbered with the most tedious tasks and most difficult clients.

Away from work, there was Tim.

Tim was a tall, dark and reasonable-looking quantity surveyor: excellent husband material, as her parents said. But, over the months they'd been going out, Tim had become more and more proprietorial.

He had strong opinions regarding her wardrobe, insisted she watched him play rugby every weekend, and criticised her driving when she provided the transport that meant he could have 'a drink or two'. He also chose the takeaways they ate and the DVDs they watched.

But while Lucy could tolerate curry when she'd really prefer Chinese, and could yawn through yet another action film knowing she'd a rom-com for his lads' night-out, what really got her goat was that, about the same time he'd begun saying they should move in together, he'd also started calling her Luce.

And that, she could not stand: it sounded somehow dismissive. Even wimps have their sticking-point.

Late one Friday morning, he rang her at work. "Pick me up at 7 for the rugby club dinner tonight. Wear your blue dress, Luce."

"It's Lucy," she said.

"Well, I know that. Who else would I think I'm talking to?"

"Got to go," she said, "Client on the other line."

It wasn't a lie - there was a client: the dreaded Denzil Barber. Smirking, Kaylie put him through.

Denzil Barber was an unpleasant go-getting property developer. "Haven't you got a tenant for my new maisonette yet?"

"There's a very nice young woman, Mr Barber," Lucy said, brightly. "Good references. Single mother with a toddler She's on universal credit but if you could reduce the rent very slightly..."

"Absolutely NOT!" he barked. "I'm not a charity. Find a proper tenant or I'll get another agency. Got that?"

He spoke so loudly, Lucy held the phone away from her ear. Andy, at the desk opposite, was listening in, grinning.

"I'll transfer you to Andy, Mr Barber," she purred, watching Andy's expression change. "He's our senior negotiator."

A press of a button and it was done. Lucy sat back, glowing with unaccustomed pleasure as she observed Andy becoming increasingly irritated, barely getting a word in edgeways. At last, he replaced the receiver.

"Why the heck d'you do that, Luce? It's not like you to be so mean."

Luce! Not him, too? She shrugged and stood up.

"I'm going for lunch," she announced, heading for the door.

She heard Kaylie whisper, "What's got into her?" Of course Lucy normally checked it was convenient to the others if she popped out - not that they reciprocated.

She strolled up the street. Eating wasn't on her agenda, with the rugby club dinner later. It would be million-calorie man-food, washed down with pints - iof water, in her case. She remembered Tim's instruction about the blue dress and felt another tsunami of annoyance. High-necked, long-sleeved and calf-length, it was far too hot for tonight. She knew Tim wanted her to wear it because a) blue was the club colour and b) while suiting her figure, it wouldn't expose anything to his team-mates' leching eyes.

A Luce dress, she thought. Well, she wouldn't wear it on his say-so. She'd buy something new. And there, in Fenshaws' window, was the answer. Oh, please let them have it in her size!

The afternoon passed quickly. Lucy got on with her work without offering to take on any extra. She sensed glances being exchanged behind her back but everyone was pleasant to her face. As Kaylie closed up, Lucy showed her the dress she'd bought.

Kaylie's eyebrows rose and jaw dropped. "Where's it you're going?"

"Rugby club dinner."

"Well, enjoy!" she said.

Lucy smiled and left. Just one more purchase to make before going home.

Lying in her bubble-bath, she giggled, recalling Kaylie's reaction to the dress and Andy's expression as he'd burbled at Denzil Barber. She'd never known a day when she'd been so assertive. She was only in the bath now because she'd finally bought one of those spider-catching vacuum gadgets.

The current interloper's thick legs had made Lucy gulp. But she'd approached courageously, long tube in shaking hand, and despite all efforts to escape, her victim was whooshed up and popped out of the window.

At last it was time for the dress: it was bright red and very short, with a neckline that plunged like an Olympic diver. Tentatively she looked in the mirror.

Pretty special, she decided.

Because of her long evening coat, which she'd buttoned, Tim didn't see her outfit until they were inside the Club. Which they'd been lucky to reach in one piece, according to him, the way she'd taken that roundabout.

As she slipped her coat off, there were several wolf-whistles.

Tim stared. "What the heck are you wearing, Luce?"

To the sound of further whistling, she replied, "I'm not Luce, I'm Lucy."

"Don't be petty," he snapped. "I want to know why my girl - my future wife - is dressed like a tart. Why red, of all colours, Luce?"

Red was what Lucy saw.

"Future wife, Tim? If that's a proposal, you can stuff it."

She grabbed her coat and marched out to cheers.

Back in her car, she didn't know whether to laugh or cry. She could hardly believe how she'd stood up for herself. Colleagues, spider, and now Tim. She'd felt braver and stronger each time and couldn't think why she'd been such a wimp for so long.

Tomorrow she'd start looking for a better job. She was going to enjoy being the new brave Lucy.

ROWS AND STITCHES

Molly holds out a ball of red yarn and two needles.

"Grandma, please can you get me started? I can't do the catching on."

"Casting on, you mean." I smile. " You catch on rather well, actually. What are you going to knit?"

"A jumper for Teddy. The scarf I made keeps his neck warm but not his tummy."

The blue garter-stitch scarf was six-year-old Molly's first go at knitting. It took a lot of time and sighing. But she did finish it, with surreptitious overnight corrections that made me feel like a shoemaker's elf, and Teddy looked the bees' knees.

"OK, poppet." I visualise something that Molly will be able to manage. Two squares back and front, two rectangles for sleeves. A button and loop on the shoulder to let it go over a large ursine head. I sketch it and she smiles her approval.

"I suppose Teddy's still lounging in bed? Go and fetch him so that I can see how many stitches to cast on."

She runs off.

I love these days when Molly's school is closed and I look after her to help my daughter and son-in-law. Now she's six, she comes the night before for a sleepover, happily skyping her parents before bedtime. All too soon, friends will be a greater draw than Grandma. But making her independent enough for that stage is what it's all about.

I was six when my Granny taught me to knit. I hadn't asked her as Molly asked me, after observing me 'magicking things' with my own needles. My Granny simply decided I should learn and no-one argued with Granny. She also taught me to say the alphabet backwards, my tables up to twelve times, make jam tarts, colour-in without going over the lines, and play shops very politely indeed. All of which I can still do today.

Granny gave me a pair of green plastic needles and a ball of something soft and bright pink. "Knitting cotton. It's shocking-pink," she said in a tone of unaccustomed naughtiness. Granny, formerly a village headmistress, was not known for naughtiness. But she had her moments. Like the shocking-pink, that 1930s colour that was rediscovered in my fifties childhood when Britain at last escaped from wartime austerity.

She cast on a dozen bright pink stitches. "Now watch, " she said. "Needle through the loop, wool round the needle, hook it through and off, and on to the next stitch. "

A pleasing scarf for my doll ensued despite the fact that my Granny never helped out overnight, but made me go back, unpick and reknit it myself until it was perfect.

Molly is back now with Teddy. I judge that thirty stitches will do. Molly looks a aghast as I cast on and on and on.

"Teddy won't like his jumper too tight, will he?" I say. "He'd have to go on a diet. No honey, no peanut butter..."

She giggles.

"There, that's enough. Shall I do the first row to get you started?"

Molly nods, and I nudge her manners. "Say 'yes, please'. My Granny would've been horrified if I'd just nodded at her."

Molly loves my tales of playing shops and all the conversations: 'Good morning, Mrs Jones.' 'Good morning, Mr Prior.' 'How can I help you, Mrs Jones?' We play the same games ourselves, even using my Granny's old kitchen scales. Molly watches carefully and chants as I start to knit: "Needle through the loop, wool round the needle ..." It's as though Granny's there too, breathing down my neck.

"There you are, then. When you've done ten rows, it'll be time for flapjack."

She sits on a stool, adorable in her flowery top and leggings, as dedicated to her work as any Victorian child sewing a sampler.

I hope these 'Grandma days' will stay bright in her memory. I think frequently of my Granny when I'm knitting - which is how I spend much of my time.

By the time I was nine, Granny had made me competent in long-division, adding up pounds, shillings and pence, toffee-making, and saying the parts of the body in French. I still know all that, though my skills in £sd are only needed in quizzes, and as for les oreilles, les dents, les genoux ... my ears, teeth and knees are trouble me more than I'd wish.

No doubt she'd have taught me much more but, quite suddenly, she was no longer bustling about telling us all what to do, but instead lay in an ugly iron bed that had squashed itself into our sitting room. There were piles of paper-wrapped dressings, dark bottles of medicine and a boxy thing called 'the commode'.

Before she got too ill, I'd go in to see her after school, trying to ignore the funny smells. I took my knitting as, once I'd answered the inevitable 'How was school today?' we had less and less to talk about. I'd long moved on from garter-stitch. I could cast on and off and do purl, I could increase and decrease and follow proper patterns. Those half-hours with Granny upped my productivity and my dolls were the best-dressed in town.

On my tenth birthday, Granny pointed to the corner cupboard, her eyes twinkling almost like they'd used to.

"There's a little present in there for you."

I edged round the bed and opened the cupboard. On the shelf were three balls of that shocking-pink knitting cotton.

That's fab, Granny! Lovely, I mean."

Together we admired the colour and the soft texture.

"I'll knit the hat from the pattern in my Princess magazine," I said, and she patted my hand.

I finished the hat, tassels and all, the day after Granny died. They'd taken her to hospital just after my birthday, and I never saw her again. Children couldn't visit in those days. They didn't let me go to the funeral, either. So I stayed at home, wearing the pink hat, while they all went out dressed in black. Mrs Davis from next door came round to look after me, tutting at my headgear. But Granny wouldn't have tutted.

In fact, I wore that hat for many years, loving it far more than my high school beret that I'd earned thanks to Granny's drilling. The pink hat, being ribbed and made of knitting cotton, obligingly stretched and lasting all through my student days. It was my trademark and everybody called me Hattie!

After school, I took a fashion degree, specialising in knitted textiles, which led to a wonderful career. Knitting is timeless, always in fashion somewhere: think layers and lace, fair isle and fringes ...

I'd learned about industrial machine knitting and began work as a designer. Later, like Granny, I became a teacher - though in a technical university. I managed to combine my work and family life. Eventually, I returned to hand-knitting, my enduring love, establishing myself as an author.

I've designed so many patterns, written so many books, that they fill the shelves above Molly's stool. Many are translated into other languages. Flicking through the French editions, words like bras gauche bring Granny's voice right back.

All of Granny's lessons have served me well. Obviously, the knitting most of all. But careful colouring-in is what's needed when planning intarsia designs. Numeracy for scaling patterns, conversion calculations and tax returns. Saying the alphabet backwards is just for showing-off (I can still do it in six seconds) and my jam tarts and toffee are a hit with Molly.

I've no intention of retiring - why, when I love what I do? I work from home, designing and authoring, and it's easily put aside for precious days with Molly.

Right now I'm working on hats again, for a new book: chunky beanies (one's in shocking pink, of course), chic berets, cabled cloches.

Suddenly I'm aware that Molly's watching me.

'What are you knitting, Grandma?'

'It's a hat that pulls down over your ears to keep them cosy. Your Mummy might like it.'

She strokes the velvety white chenille that I'm using. "Will there be some left for me to make Teddy a hat ?

"Perhaps when you've finished his jumper. How are you getting on?

"Very well." She holds up her work hopefully.

"You've done five rows," I say. "And you're knitting really well." It's true - no dropped stitches, nothing for the knitting elf so far. "Let's have our drink and flapjack now. You've worked so hard, you deserve it."

She beams.

I head for the kitchen. "Will knitting be as important in your life as it's been in mine, I wonder?"

I don't realise I've spoken aloud. But Molly's heard all right, and her reply is pretty surprising from a six-year-old.

"You never know where things end up, Grandma, once you get started."

"Wherever did you get that from?" I hug her. "You sound just like my wise old Granny.'

STIR-UP SUNDAY

S ue battled her way through the Saturday shopping crowds. Still five weeks until Christmas, yet already everybody was buying crazily.

'Buy now, pay later' adverts splattered the shop windows. But much as Sue liked a traditional Christmas, she'd never dream of getting into debt for it. Money had often been tight when the children were small, but she and Jim just cut back. The kids always got a nice present and, if there was ever disappointment over not having the latest blockbuster toy, they soon forgot when they realised few of their friends had the coveted item either.

The 'kids' were nineteen and seventeen now, Chloe on a gap-year and Jack just started in the 6th form. They'd both requested money for their 'big' present this year, Chloe texting from Melbourne, the latest stopping-point on her version of a world tour.

Sue could see Chloe's reasoning - what else could they do, when she was halfway round the world? But she'd tackled Jack. "Are you sure, love? Surprises get scarce enough when you're older. Your dad …" but she stopped, not wanting to be critical. Jim wasn't mean, just unimaginative. He handed Sue a wadge of notes every birthday and Christmas saying, "Choose yourself something nice." But Sue couldn't help wishing he'd sometimes surprise her.

Jack shrugged, twanging his guitar. "I'd rather have money than something I don't want. Too much fuss, Christmas."

He was right: Christmas was too much fuss. It took over everything, just for a few days' relentless eating, drinking and consumer indulgence.

Sue had always loved stuffing the children's stockings, though.

She'd kept the tradition going, using the same red stockings they had when they were tiny.

It was stocking presents she'd been buying today. For all Jack might make a face, she thought he'd be pleased really - and his requested cash would be there, stuffed into the toe. And Chloe's stocking? It would just have to stay full, waiting until she got home again.

Sue tried to suppress the stabbing sadness she felt at the prospect of not having Chloe home for Christmas. Whilst admiring her daughter's confidence and enterprise, she'd missed her badly ever since her departure in August. But what nineteen-year-old wouldn't want to see the world? She was meeting all sorts of people - nice ones, Sue prayed fervently - and finding work here and there to pay her way. India and Japan had already been ticked off. Now Australia, next New Zealand some time around February.

Great stuff for my CV, Mum, Chloe texted.

The stocking was one of Sue's ways of coping: grim determination mixed with mental fast-forwarding to when she got home again.

It was much harder finding stocking fillers at Chloe and Jack's ages. When they were little, cheap and cheerful presents did nicely: bubble-bath in animal-shaped bottles, plastic dinosaurs and trumpets.

Thank goodness their stockings were a reasonable size, not huge sacks. Today, she'd snapped up earrings for Chloe, and cosmetics, hoping she still liked the same brands. Guitar strings for Jack, plus bodyspray and a snazzy alarm clock. Sweets, chocolate, diaries for both of them. And she'd just found frog and cat bath mitts in the pound shop. Those had made her smile.

Preoccupied by tallying her purchases, Sue almost bumped into a giant plum pudding on legs.

"Sorry..."

"Madam, take a recipe sheet," the pudding boomed, a sprig of holly bobbing wildly on his head. "You can buy all the ingredients here in Healtharama." The pudding gestured towards the health food store behind him.

The shop window proclaimed STIR UP SUNDAY. Wasn't that about making wishes? Not a tradition they followed in their family. Sue always bought a pudding. Still, a wonderful smell of spices drifted from the door and the gleaming raisins and nuts in the window made her mouth water.

Why not? Jim would no doubt enjoy a homemade Christmas pudding and everybody could do with a wish coming true.

She went into the shop.

On Sunday morning, Jack surfaced reluctantly from a dream in which he and Lizzie Williams were doing something very delectable. He shook his head sadly, yawned, then brightened as he sniffed the air. Mmm. Roast dinner. Good old Mum! Humming a catch of the wistful song he was midway through composing – it was called Beautiful Lizzie – he stepped into the clothes he'd left strategically-placed on the floor then, taking the stairs two at a time, reached the kitchen in ten seconds.

"Hey, Mum, what's for breakfast?"

"Whatever you can scavenge, Jack. You can see I'm up to my eyes."

He looked. Ginormous mixing bowl, worktop covered in flour, packets of currants and stuff ... it was like a horror scene from a food technology room.

"That's not dinner, is it?"

"No, you dope. Dinner's in the oven. Can't you smell it? This is Christmas pudding. Today's Stir Up Sunday. Everybody stirs the mixture and makes a secret wish. You can be first."

Jack was by now rooting in the breadbin. "Do I have to?"

"No. I just thought we'd try a new tradition this Christmas. Don't bother, if there's nothing you want to wish for."

Jack frowned. Typical Mum idea, this. But ... it'd need something magic to make Lizzie come to the Year 12 Christmas party with him, when she was going out with George. He put down the baguette and took the wooden spoon.

When Jim entered the kitchen, he was carrying the fat Sunday paper he'd bought on his Sunday morning constitutional.

"Hey, that cake smells good!"

"It's Christmas pudding." Sue added more spice to the heavy mixture. "I fancied making some this year."

"Not for today, then?" A crestfallen look.

"Certainly not. But only five weeks to wait. And now you're here, have a stir and make a wish."

"A wish? What for?"

"That's up to you. But keep it secret. And you never know, it might come true."

Jim scratched his head. Sue had funny ideas sometimes. But there was something he wished: that he could find a really nice Christmas present for Sue. To help make up for Chloe being away. But whatever would Sue really like?

"Give me the spoon, then," he said.

"All yours," said Sue. "And while you give it a really good stir, I'll get the potatoes on."

As he stirred, Jim tried to imagine Sue smiling as she opened a present he'd just handed to her. He wished hard for inspiration.

77

The Stir Up Sunday idea had gone down pretty well with her men-folk, thought Sue. Three full pudding basins stood on the work-top. After lunch, she'd boil them. The warm spicy smell would fill the house all day.

But first - or rather, last - it was Sue's turn. Even if it was all non-sense, she would make a really serious wish, from the bottom of her heart. A wish so special that it would make or break Christ-mas, depending on whether or not it came true.

F ive weeks later, Sue woke up early to Christmas Day. With both sets of grandparents coming for the day, and a family-sized turkey to cook, she was going to be busy.

As she slipped out of bed, Jim rolled over.

"It's OK, you can go back to sleep," she told him, putting on her dressing gown and closing the door behind her.

In his room across the landing, she could hear Jack singing quietly. It was unusually early for him to be awake. But Sue, hearing the words 'Sweet Lizzie' in the haunting melody, knew why. He'd been on cloud nine ever since that school party, when he and the Lizzie of the song had become an item. Now whenever he was not actually with the said Lizzie, they seemed to be texting one an-other non-stop.

Sue tapped on his door. "Merry Christmas, Jack".

The singing stopped and a gruff voice replied. "Hey, Mum - Merry Christmas! And thanks for the stocking. I never thought you'd bother this year."

Sue put her head round. Jack was sitting up in bed, his duvet festooned with Christmas paper and all the things she'd painstak-ingly wrapped only hours earlier, placing the stocking beside his bed some time past midnight.

"Of course I'd bother. Wouldn't be Christmas without a stocking, would it?"

"No way. Lizzie just texted. Her mum did her a stocking too," he grinned. "And thanks specially for the dosh in the toe. Your prezzie's under the tree, by the way."

He put his arms out for a hug and Sue breathed in the inimitable teenage boy smell of skin and cotton and toothpaste and goodness knows what. At least she was definitely hugging one of her children this Christmas Day.

Jim opened his eyes properly, hearing the muted conversation. Tempting as it was, he wouldn't doze off again. Not fair to leave everything to Sue, with a houseful to cook for. Anyway, he was excited - if nervous - at the prospect of seeing Sue's reaction to his surprise. That Sunday - what did Sue call it? Stirring Sunday? - no sooner had he made his wish than it came true! The magazine section of his paper had been full of present ideas. Things he'd never have thought of. He just hoped Sue would like what he'd chosen.

Waiting for the kettle to boil, Sue mentally planned her cooking timetable. Turkey, stuffing, pigs-in-blankets, loads of veg and, of course, the pudding . She thought back to Stir Up Sunday and the wish-making. She was pretty sure what Jack had wished for, now she saw him in love for the first time. But Jim? What did grown men wish for? Sports cars? Early retirement?

As for her own wish, she'd thought about it every day since. She looked at the clock. Soon, surely ...

"Oh!..."

Jim had padded up behind her and was pulling her into a big embrace.

"Happy Christmas, sweetheart. Here, for you."

Surprised, Sue took the small gift-wrapped parcel.

"But ..."

"I know ... I always say choose something yourself. Well, you deserve better, especially this year ... with Chloe away." He looked rather anxious. "Open it, then."

"Now? Whatever is it?" Sue pulled the ribbons undone to reveal a blue velvet box ... inside, encased in white satin, an opal pendant and matching earrings.

"Oh, Jim, they're just beautiful. What a wonderful surprise."

"I thought ... opals come from Australia. You ought to have something coming from Australia this Christmas ..."

"Maybe not the only thing."

As Sue wiped away a tear and fastened the pendant around her neck, the Waltzing Matilda ringtone of her mobile chimed out.

"Quick!" Sue raced to the lounge to switch on her laptop on the coffee table. "That's Chloe's warning to say she's on Skype. Call Jack!"

Almost instantly, Chloe's face beamed from the screen.

"Chloe, darling! Happy Christmas!"

"Hey Mum, Dad. Merry Christmas to you. It's really weird saying that in this temperature. I'm just off to a beach barbie with the hostel crowd. There'll be turkey and stuff. Gotta keep up some traditions."

"We're keeping them all," Sue said, holding up Chloe's stocking. "For when you come back."

Momentarily, Chloe looked sad. "Oh, I miss you," she said.

"I bet you do," Jack laughed, "with all that sun, sea and surfing."

"True," Chloe beamed again. "Honestly, it's awesome here. "

By eleven, the older generation had arrived, bearing armfuls of presents.

Sue's Dad was the first to mention the unmentionable: "We've brought Chloe's present. It's not the same without her, eh, Sue? You must be longing for her to walk through that door."

Sue swallowed. "It's OK. Of course we miss her, but we talked on Skype this morning. Late afternoon there, of course. She's having a fantastic time in Melbourne."

She bent to arrange the parcels under the Christmas tree. They'd open them after lunch – in fact, after the pudding - as was their tradition.

"Chloe looked really happy," Sue continued. "And I couldn't wish for anything else, could I?"

ABOUT THE AUTHOR

Liz Summerson

Liz has written stories and poems for publication in women's magazines and as entries to competitions over many years.

Liz grew up in the beautiful county of Herefordshire and has since lived in Brighton, Huddersfield and Wiltshire. She has been married to Rob since 1972. She has a BA Hons in History (University of Sussex, MA in Creative Writing (University of Bath Spa) and the full Diploma in French from the Institute of Liinguists. She worked for many years in careers advisory services, including publications, and has taught French to adults for 17 years.

Her current interests include family and social history, Scrabble, cats, painting, handcrafts, learning Spanish, and town twinning. She has been a governor of a local comprehensive school for 25 years and is passionate about equal rights and opportunities.

MORE SHORT STORIES BY LIZ SUMMERSON

The Perfect Strangers And Other Stories

Printed in Great Britain
by Amazon